The Rowdy Rooster

Farmer Claude and Farmer Maude
were asleep on a Sunday morning.
The sheep, the dog, the goat, and hog
were woken without warning.

The rowdy rooster crowed out loud
just as the day was dawning.
It was such a shock, at 5 o'clock –
too early in the morning.

He woke the sheep.

He woke the dog.

He woke the goat.

He woke the hog.

4

"I need *my* sleep," bleated the sheep,

and the dog just barked where he lay.

The goat stamped his feet and bared his teeth,

and the hog shook his head in dismay.

Farmer Claude and Farmer Maude

were woken with a shock.

Farmer Maude looked at the time and cried, "It's five o'clock!"

"What should we do?"

cried Farmer Claude.

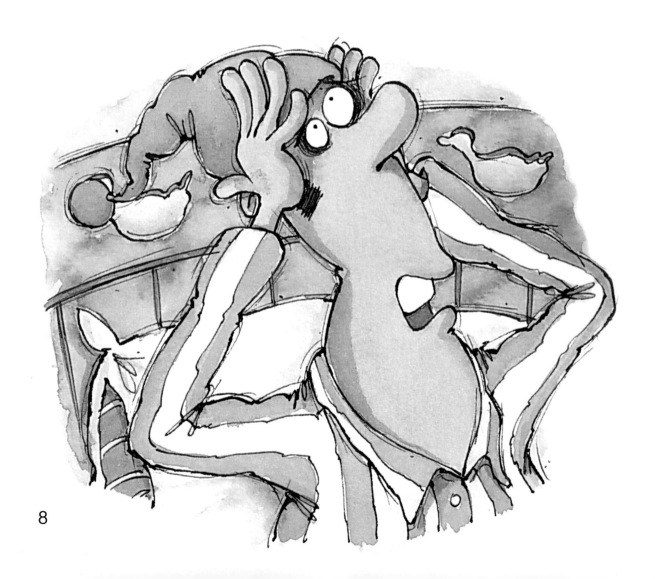

8

"I have a plan!"

cried Farmer Maude.

So Farmer Claude and Farmer Maude
walked to the big red shed.

The sheep, the dog, the goat, and hog
followed where they led.

"Look at that bed!" the farmers said.

"There are bits of straw.

There are bits of sticks.

There are bits of wood.

There are bits of bricks!"

"No wonder the rooster doesn't sleep,"
baaed the tired sheep.
The dog just yawned, the goat bared his teeth,
and the hog huddled up in a heap.

"It's time for your plan!"

cried Farmer Claude.

"It's shearing time!"

cried Farmer Maude.

So Farmer Claude and Farmer Maude
got scissors from out of the shed.
With a snip and a snap and a snippety-snap,
they were making that rooster a bed.

They sheared the sheep.

They clipped the dog.

They plucked the goat.

They snipped the hog.

Farmer Claude and Farmer Maude

made that rooster a bed.

"This will keep our rooster asleep.

It's warm and cuddly," they said.

19

The very next morning, as day was dawning, the farmers woke with a shock.

"Tick-tock, tick-tock!" said the farmhouse clock.

It was nearly 5 o'clock!

Farmer Claude and Farmer Maude
walked to the big red shed.
There inside the rooster snored,
still sleeping on his bed.

"Zzz-zz," snored the sheep.

"Zzz-zz," snored the dog.

"Zzz-zz," snored the goat.

"Zzz-zz," snored the hog.

23

Farmer Claude and Farmer Maude
watched them sleeping, too.
Then Farmer Claude and Farmer Maude
crowed, "COCK-A-DOODLE-DOO!"

24